JAKE'S CAVE

LOU KUENZLER

ILLUSTRATED BY

NICK MALAND

WALKER
BOOKS

For Paul with the Beard –
thanks for all the magical trips
L.K.

For Tess, Alan and Eleanor
N.M.

This is a work of fiction. Names, characters, places and incidents are either the product of the author's imagination or, if real, are used fictitiously. All statements, activities, stunts, descriptions, information and material of any other kind contained herein are included for entertainment purposes only and should not be relied on for accuracy or replicated, as they may result in injury.

First published 2010 by Walker Books Ltd
87 Vauxhall Walk, London SE11 5HJ

2 4 6 8 10 9 7 5 3

This book has been typeset in Bembo Educational and Alpha Bold

Printed and bound in China

British Library Cataloguing in Publication Data:
a catalogue record for this book is available from the British Library

ISBN: 978-1-4063-2153-1

www.walker.co.uk

Something Sensible

It was half-term. Mum and Dad had to go to work.

"Why don't I take the children out for a treat?" suggested Uncle Paul.

"Brilliant!" Jake grinned. Spending time with his favourite uncle was always fun.

Uncle Paul flipped a coin high in the air. "If this lands on heads, Pip can choose the treat," he said. "Tails, and it's up to Jake."

"Fairy World!" cried Pip.

But the coin landed on tails.

Jake knew at once where he wanted to go. "Windy Beach!" he said. Uncle Paul had taken him there once before, when Pip was just a tiny baby.

"Good choice," agreed Uncle Paul.

"There's a HUGE cave, hidden deep in the cliffs," Jake told Pip, spreading his arms wide to show her how big it was. "It's the best place in the world to hunt for treasure!"

But Pip stuck out her tongue. "Yuck," she said. "Smelly cave."

"Don't come, then!" said Jake with a mischievous grin. "But if you don't, you won't see the dragon…"

"What dragon?" asked Pip, her eyes wide and curious.

"The dragon who lives in the cave," explained Jake. He knew dragons weren't real, of course. He was only pretending. Just for Pip.

"It's a girl dragon," he invented.

He knew his little sister would like that. "She's as big as a bus and bright red. As red and shiny as your new wellies!"

Pip loved her wellies and ran to pull them on. "Go now! Go now!" she begged.

"Hold on! You can't go to the beach in your nightie," laughed Uncle Paul.

"You need to wear something sensible."

That was pretty funny, considering Uncle Paul was wearing silly baggy shorts with blue lobsters on them.

But Pip looked as though she might cry.

Oh no, thought Jake. This was no time for a tantrum, or they'd never get to the beach. Quick as a superhero, he flew upstairs. "Come on, Pip," he shouted down. "There'll be something in the dressing-up box that's just right for visiting a dragon!"

Jake tipped the costumes out onto the bedroom floor. There were bat wings and clown trousers; Cinderella slippers and gorilla gloves. There was also a slimy grey wetsuit that used to belong to Dad.

Jake flung the suit around his shoulders and wobbled his arms like a giant squid. "You could dive to the bottom of the sea and look for sunken ships in this," he said.

But Pip shook her head and frowned.

"How about my pirate costume?" asked Jake. "Pirates love the seaside!" He hopped about with a patch over one eye, pretending he was Peg Leg Jake. "Shiver me timbers, Pirate Pip!" he chuckled, but Pip shook her head again.

She went over to the box and dug out a bright pink tutu and a pink and purple furry cloak, which she pulled on. She added a sparkly gold tiara and began to twirl around in her wellies. "I am a ballerina princess," she sang. "I will dance for the dragon in her cave."

"Don't you know anything?" sighed Jake. "Dragons eat princesses! Dressed like that, you'll be gobbled up in one gulp."

"The dragon won't eat me, silly," laughed Pip. She picked up a knight's helmet and a chain-mail vest and gave them to Jake. "YOU will protect me, brave knight!"

Jake grinned. The knight's costume was one of his favourites. "I suppose I *could* wear these," he said. "We are going to a dragon's cave, after all."

He strapped on the armour, grabbed his sword and charged back down the stairs. "Beware, dragon! I am Sir Jake the Brave!" he roared.

He lunged at the tablecloth,
then turned to fight
a fierce mop
and bucket.

Uncle Paul raised his eyebrows. "I thought you were going to wear something sensible?"

"This *is* sensible … for a dragon hunt," Jake explained.

"Of course!" laughed Uncle Paul, waving his stripy beach umbrella like a lance. "Lead on, Sir Jake! Lead on to the dragon's cave!"

Jake mounted his imaginary horse
and charged out to the car.

He was only pretending
to be a knight, of course.

Just for Princess Pip!

Are We Nearly There Yet?

Jake and Pip scrambled into the back of Uncle Paul's bright red sports car.

"Let's have the top down," said Uncle Paul, sliding open the roof. He knew this was the first thing Jake would ask.

"Hold on to your tiara, Pip," grinned Jake as they sped off. "It might blow away!" He tightened the strap on his knight's helmet.

At the end of the road they drove past Jake's school. The playground was empty because it was half-term. Jake wished his friends were there so they could see him in Uncle Paul's fast car.

They flew round six roundabouts and through seven sets of green traffic lights. Jake made car noises and pretended to drive, spinning an imaginary steering wheel and changing gear.

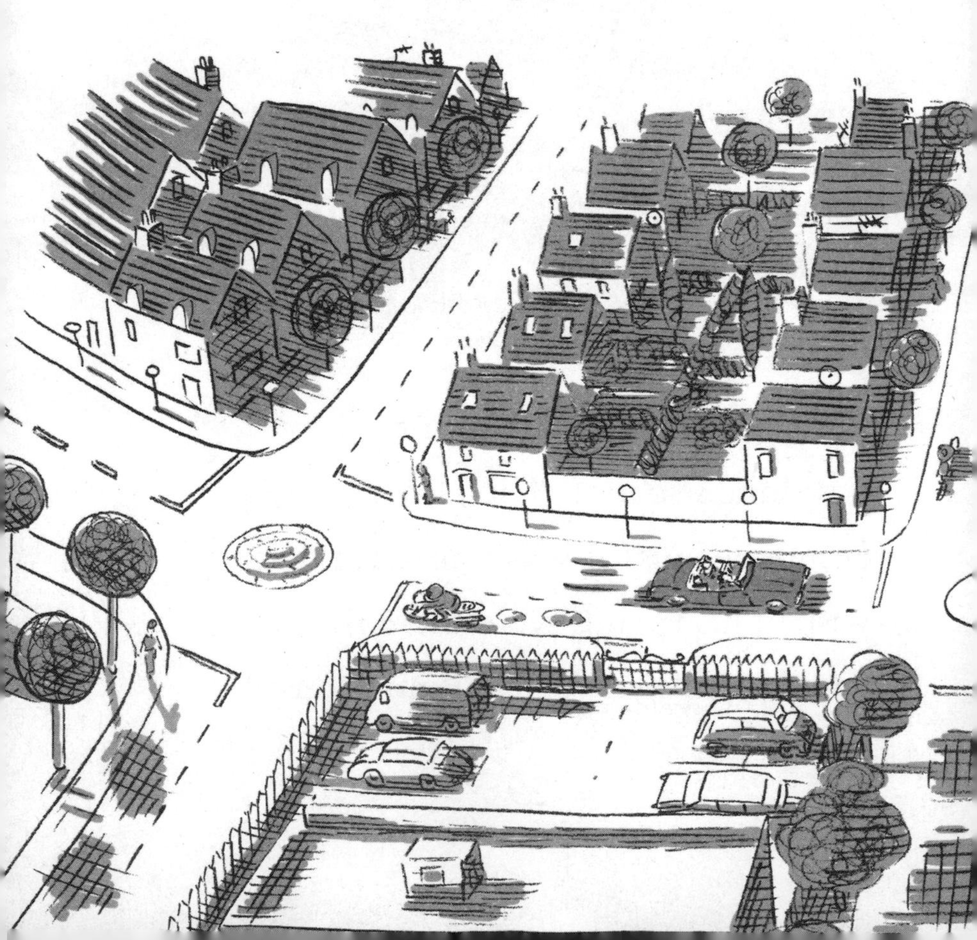

But Pip was bored already. "Are we nearly there yet?" she whined.

"Not quite," said Uncle Paul.

Jake knew they still had a long, long way to go.

Now they had to travel for miles down the motorway. "Let's count cars," suggested Jake to pass the time more quickly. "I'll count silver ones, like knights in shining armour."

"Good idea! I'll count big red buses, like your dragon," said Uncle Paul.

"What about me?" wailed Pip.

"You can be pink," said Jake. "Pink cars are for princesses going to a ball!"

But there were no pink cars … or big red buses.

Pip got cross. "Stupid game," she said.

"One hundred and twenty-two!" cheered Jake as they left the motorway. "Silver cars win."

"We're not playing any more!" said Pip and Uncle Paul together.

Jake kept counting, but it wasn't any fun on his own.

"Not much further," announced Uncle Paul, turning down one of the winding roads that led to the sea.

“Smell that salty air! We’ll be at the beach in no time.”

But a farmer and his cows were blocking the lane ahead.

Now even Jake was fed up. "This is taking for ever," he moaned. He wished the cows were aliens from outer space, then they could zap back to another planet. "Go and visit the stars!" he called to them. "You could see the *Milky* Way!"

"Moo!" nodded a cow, but she didn't hurry.

At last the farmer waved Uncle Paul through. A black and white farm dog barked loudly as they passed.

"Look, Pip!" said Jake. "It's a collie."

Black and white collies were Pip's favourite kind of dog – but she was fast asleep.

"It's a pity she missed it," said Uncle Paul.

Jake pushed his feet against the seat in front of him and sighed. He felt stiff and tired from sitting in the car so long. If only they were at the beach right now!

Then Jake saw it – a shimmer of sea, sparkling bright blue in the sun.

"Look, Pip," he whispered, shaking her awake.

Pip blinked. "Are we nearly there yet?" she yawned.

"YES!" cheered Jake and Uncle Paul together.

"I need a wee," said Pip.

"And I need a coffee," said Uncle Paul.

Jake groaned.

First he had to wait for Pip to go to the toilet and wash her hands, *then* for Uncle Paul to talk to the café man about the traffic.

"Come *on*," begged Jake. "PLEASE!"

"All right, Sir Jake the Brave, let's race," said Uncle Paul, and he grabbed Pip's hand.

The three of them charged down the beach together. The wind whistled through Jake's helmet and blew Pip's cloak out behind her.

"Look, Pip!" cried Jake, pointing to a cloud above the cliffs. "That's the dragon's smoke. She's breathing fire in her cave!" He was really excited now. He remembered how deep and dark and dangerous the cave had been.

Pip looked a little worried. "Are we nearly there yet?" she stammered.

Jake realized in surprise that they were. Last time it had felt like a long walk to the cave ... but the beach seemed shorter now.

"Yes!" he said. "We're there!"

At the Cave

As soon as Jake saw the cave, his heart sank. It was much smaller than he had remembered.

But Pip gasped. "Is that where the dragon lives?" she whispered, peeping out from behind Jake's legs.

"I suppose so," he said, although he didn't feel like playing any more.

It wasn't a cave at all, really, just a little hollow in the rocks. Someone as small as Pip might squeeze inside. But not Jake.

Pip pushed him forward. "You go first," she said, hiding behind him. "I'm MUCH too scared!"

"Get off!" snapped Jake, disappointed that the cave was so small. His legs ached from running along the beach and he felt sick from the long car journey. All that way, he thought, just for this?

"Come on, Sir Jake," coaxed Uncle Paul. "You've got a dragon to find. Lead on!"

Jake poked his head through the narrow crack in the rocks. The gap was barely wide enough for his shoulders to fit through.

The cave was tiny.

Jake could see the back wall. There certainly wasn't any treasure – not even anything the tide had washed up. There were just a few large stones, that was all.

"Is the dragon in there?" Pip's voice echoed behind him.

Jake stepped back. "See for yourself. I'm too big to fit inside." He threw the knight's helmet on the ground.

"I can't go in on my own," shivered Pip. "Dragons eat princesses!"

Uncle Paul picked up the helmet, giving Jake a stern look. "I'll protect you if Jake won't," he said.

Jake felt a mean feeling twist in his tummy. His face felt hot and red. It wasn't fair. The cave was stupid and small. He was too big to fit, and now Pip was having all the fun! She was screaming and giggling, hiding behind her cloak.

Uncle Paul balanced the helmet on his head. "I am Uncle Sir Paul the Brave!" he thundered, opening his beach umbrella like a shield.

"Stop it!" shouted Jake. "There isn't any dragon!" The mean feeling crashed like waves inside him. "It was just pretend. I made it up!"

"Jake!" said Uncle Paul.

But Jake ran off. He sat down by the water, throwing stones into the sea.

"Stupid cave," he muttered. He didn't even look back to see if Pip had gone inside.

After a while Uncle Paul came and sat beside him.

"It's a long time since we visited this beach," he said. "You were younger than Pip when I brought you here."

"Was I?" sulked Jake.

"You've grown," said Uncle Paul. "That's why everything seems smaller now."

"It's a stupid, tiny cave," grumbled Jake. "I wish it was big, like I remember it."

"The cave was never big," said Uncle Paul, "but your imagination is!" He put the knight's helmet back on Jake's head. "Your imagination made that cave big enough for a dragon. A dragon as big as a bus," he grinned.

Jake looked back at the cave. Pip was struggling across the stones towards them. She was carrying something in her arms.

“This is for you, Jake!” she called. “I found it in the cave.” She held out a large grey rock. “Is it treasure?” she asked.

Jake stared at the rock. It was smooth all over and speckled with green spots. "No, that isn't treasure," he said.

Pip looked so disappointed that the mean feeling left him, like waves slipping back out to sea.

Jake smiled. "That's much better than treasure. That's … a dragon's egg!"

Pip gasped. *"Really?"*

Jake nodded, catching Uncle Paul's eye. "The dragon must have laid it before she flew away," he said.

"Are you pretending?" asked Pip. "Just for me?"

Jake shook his head. “Of course not, Pip. An egg like that will hatch into a dragon as big as a bus,” he told her. “Just you wait and see!”